Her Mother's Face

Her Mother's Face

RODDY DOYLE

Illustrated by
FREYA BLACKWOOD

First published in 2008 by Scholastic Inc
This paperback edition first published in the UK in 2009 by Scholastic Children's Books
Euston House, 24 Eversholt Street
London NW1 1DB, UK
a division of Scholastic Ltd
www.scholastic.co.uk
London ~ New York ~ Toronto ~ Sydney ~ Auckland
Mexico City ~ New Delhi ~ Hong Kong

ISBN 978 1407 10787 5

1 3 5 7 9 10 8 6 4 2

Dedicated to my mother, Ita Doyle ~
R.D.

To Katie and Ivy ~
F.B.

SCHOLASTIC

There was once this girl and her name was Siobhán. She lived in a big house in Dublin with her father. It was a great house, full of interesting rooms and corners, full of old magazines and old machines and old, old toys and teddy bears. Siobhán spent hours and hours exploring the rooms and halls, and she always found something new. She loved the house.

Her mother had died when Siobhán was only three. She had no sisters and no brothers, no uncles, aunts, or cousins, and no grandparents. There was just Siobhán and her father. He was a nice man, but he was very quiet and sad, and he kept himself to himself. He read to Siobhán sometimes. He brought her home a new book every Friday. He smiled whenever he saw her looking at him, but he never spoke to her about her mother. In fact, nobody ever spoke to Siobhán about her mother.

Siobhán was ten now, and she could not remember her mother's face. She had searched every corner of the house. She found her mother's old books and a scarf and a pair of mad green shoes, but she never found a photograph.

Siobhán could remember her mother's hands. Her hands combing Siobhán's hair, her hands peeling an apple, holding the steering wheel, pulling up Siobhán's sock, and her hands on her lap when Siobhán was brought into the dark room to say good-bye to her. When Siobhán closed her eyes, she could see her mother's hands doing these things and other things but, no matter how hard she tried or how long she kept her eyes closed, she couldn't see her mother's face.

She could remember her mother's voice. And she could remember some words.

"Cat and spuds for dinner, Siobhán. How does that sound?"

"Yeuk."

"Yeuk, cat? Or yeuk, spuds?"

"Yeuk, cat."

"Okay. We'll have chicken instead."

And she could remember her mother singing, "Did you ever shove your granny off the bus?" She could hear her mother, but she could never see her face.

The empty space where her mother's face should have been was like a pain, a giant unhappiness that Siobhán carried with her everywhere.

When she saw other mothers hugging their children, or buttoning their coats, and even when she saw her friends' mothers yelling at her friends, the pain grew in her chest and pushed up tears to her eyes. And, as she got older, the pain got worse and worse, because her mother seemed to be going further and further away.

Other children liked Siobhán. They liked sitting beside her in school. She never argued, and she never whinged or grabbed and broke things. She made them laugh. She would cross her eyes and say the things that adults love saying.

"Money doesn't grow on trees."

"It's raining cats and dogs."

"I have eyes in the back of my head."

Her friends all knew that Siobhán's mother was dead, but none of them knew how sad she was. She never told them, and she never let them see.

When she tried to talk to her father about her mother, his face would fill with worry and sadness, and she'd stop. He hugged her once and said, "Sorry." They had a pizza and watched telly together. It was nice, but they didn't talk.

One day, Siobhán was sitting in Saint Anne's Park, very near her house. She sat under a huge chestnut tree. She could remember her mother's hands holding her up, high enough to pull a conker from the lowest branch. She could remember the voice.

"The big one, the big one. Grab it. Yesss!"

She could remember how it felt, the hands squeezing through her coat and dress, the nice safe feeling, knowing that she wouldn't fall. She tried to remember turning to smile at her mother, but she couldn't. This was what Siobhán was doing, trying to remember, when she heard a voice.

"Hello."

Siobhán looked and saw a beautiful woman standing beside her. The woman sat straight down on the grass. Most adults never did this, because it was quite mucky and damp.

"You're sad, aren't you?" said the beautiful woman.

She had dark brown hair, like Siobhán's, and brown eyes. And she had a friendly smile and a lovely voice. Siobhán never spoke to strangers, but this woman didn't seem like a stranger.

"Yes," said Siobhán. "I am sad. A bit."

"Why?" said the woman.

And Siobhán told her. She told her everything. About her mother's death, and her hands, and about how she could never see her mother's face. And she cried as she spoke, but she didn't mind. She just kept talking.

The woman listened, and smiled.

"You know what you should do?" she said when Siobhán had finished talking.

"What?" said Siobhán.

The woman wiped Siobhán's eyes with the sleeve of her jumper.

"You should look in the mirror," said the woman.

"Why?" said Siobhán.

"Because then you'll see your mother," said the woman. "You'll see the way she looked when she was your age. And, as you get older, you'll see what your mother looked like when she was getting older."

Then she kissed Siobhán, and hugged her.

"How's your daddy?" she said.

"He's fine," said Siobhán. "But he's very sad too."

"Give him a message from me," said the woman. "Tell him — "

And she whispered the message into Siobhán's ear.

Siobhán laughed.

"Why?" she said.

"Just tell him, and then *he'll* tell you," said the woman. And then she stood up.

"Goodbye, Siobhán," said the woman.

"We'll meet again, I'm sure."

She walked away, out of the park.

Siobhán went home and went to the bathroom and looked in the mirror. At first, all she could see was her own face. But she stayed there, looking. And, after a few minutes, she began to imagine another girl, very like herself, but not exactly the same. The hair a little different, the mouth a little smaller, the lips a little darker. And she could make her look a little older, and a little more. And Siobhán knew. She was able to imagine her mother's face.

She closed her eyes. She could feel her mother's hands holding her up to grab the conker. She turned, and she could see her mother's face. It wasn't clear, it wasn't exact. But it was there, in her head.

"The big one, the big one. Grab it. Yesss!"

And Siobhán felt happy for the first time since her mother had died. But she forgot all about the beautiful woman's message to her father.

Siobhán grew older – fourteen, fifteen. She looked in the mirror every morning and evening. Everybody noticed and thought that Siobhán was admiring her own beauty. But nobody minded, because Siobhán *was* beautiful. Eighteen, nineteen, twenty. More years passed, and Siobhán now had a little girl of her own, called Ellen, Siobhán's mother's name.

One day, on the morning of her thirtieth birthday, Siobhán put on her mother's mad green shoes because it was a special day. Then she went with Ellen to visit her father in the big house. Her father brought Ellen for a walk in Saint Anne's. While they were away, Siobhán went upstairs to the bathroom. She looked into the mirror and got a shock. She was looking straight at the beautiful woman she'd met all those years ago in the park. The beautiful woman had been her mother, and now, on her birthday, Siobhán looked exactly like her.

She cried.

She heard the front door slamming and little Ellen ran into the bathroom. She was holding a conker. She stopped when she saw Siobhán.

"Why are you crying, Mammy?" she said.

Siobhán picked her up.

"Sometimes people cry when they're happy," said Siobhán.

"Can I cry as well then?" said Ellen.

"Yes, love," said Siobhán.

And Siobhán and Ellen cried until they were soaking wet and laughing.

Siobhán's father walked into the bathroom. He had heard them crying, and he looked worried. Suddenly, Siobhán remembered her mother's message, the words she had whispered into her ear all those years ago.

"Put a feather in your knickers, Dad," she said.

Ellen laughed.

Her father's face went very pale.

"Where did you hear that?" he said.

"A beautiful woman told me to tell you," said Siobhán.

"Your mother," said her father. "She said it to me whenever she thought I was being too serious."

"Put a feather in your knickers, Granda," said Ellen.

And he laughed. It was the first time Siobhán had heard him laugh. They went downstairs and made coffee and Siobhán's father told them all about her mother, Ellen's grandmother.

He told them about how they'd met – at a bus stop on Abbey Street. He told them about the first film they'd gone to see together, *Revenge of the Killer Snails*. She loved it, he hated it, and she shoved a piece of popcorn up his nose. He told them about their wedding day – how the cake fell off the table when they were trying to cut it. He told them everything. It was dark by the time he stopped talking. He was tired, and he was happy. Siobhán was also very tired and happy. And little Ellen was asleep.

And that's the end of the story.
Siobhán didn't live happily ever after, but
she lived a long, long life, and she was happy a lot
of the time. Her father lived enough to see Ellen grow
into a woman.

And what about Ellen? She's mad and funny and beautiful, and she cycles around Dublin with a big bag of feathers, looking for men who look too serious.